Enid Blyton

TOYLAND STORIES

Brer Rabbit and the Potato Fight

This edition published in 2000 by Diamond Books
77-85 Fulham Palace Road
Hammersmith, London, W68JB

First published in Great Britain by HarperCollins Publishers Ltd in 1998

1 3 5 7 9 10 8 6 4 2

Copyright © 1998 Enid Blyton Company Ltd. Enid Blyton's
signature mark and the word 'TOYLAND' are Registered Trade Marks of Enid Blyton Ltd.
For further information on Enid Blyton please contact www.blyton.com

ISBN: 0 00 761011 4

Printed and bound in Italy
Colour Reproduction by Dot Gradations Ltd U.K.

Enid Blyton™

TOYLAND™ STORIES

Brer Rabbit and the Potato Fight

CARNIVAL

One day, Brer Rabbit popped his head over Brer Fox's fence, and saw Brer Fox digging up potatoes.

"Those are fine potatoes," said Brer Rabbit.

Brer Fox laughed. "I hear your potatoes are all bad," he said, "but don't think you can have any of mine."

"Keep your potatoes," said Brer Rabbit crossly. "I don't want them."

"I'll let you have one," said Brer Fox, and he picked up a potato and threw it hard at Brer Rabbit. It hit him on the nose, and he squealed and fell over.

Brer Fox rolled on the ground with laughter.

"What a good shot!" he cried. "Right on Brer Rabbit's nose!"

Brer Rabbit went off through the wood, rubbing his nose where the potato had hit it. He was very angry with Brer Fox, and he was determined to get some of those potatoes.

By the time Brer Rabbit had reached home, he had thought of a crafty plan to outwit Brer Fox, and he called to his wife and children, "Come on, we're going out to have some fun, but first you must all find a bonnet or a hat to wear."

Mrs Rabbit and the children were puzzled, but they scurried about to find all kinds of hats, old and new. There were bonnets and hats and caps, and Brer Rabbit even found a top hat that looked very funny on his furry head.

"Now listen," said Brer Rabbit. "We're going to get enough potatoes from Brer Fox's garden to make potato soup for tonight's supper."

"How will we do that?" squeaked the youngest rabbit.

"Well," said Brer Rabbit, "Brer Fox has just hit me on the nose with a potato and he was so pleased with himself that I think he'll have a shot at anyone who passes. If we walk past

his garden with our hats showing above his fence, I'm sure
he'll have a go at hitting us with his potatoes. Then we'll
pick up the potatoes and run home as fast as we can."

"But the children are too small," said Mrs Rabbit.
"Their heads won't reach the top of the fence."

"Then they must hold their hats on a stick!" said
Brer Rabbit.

The little rabbits were very excited and scampered off to find sticks. Then they all set off to Brer Fox's house.

"Shh!" said Brer Rabbit, as they came near to Brer Fox's house. "There's the fence that runs alongside his potato patch."

"You wait here, children," said Mrs Rabbit. "Your father and I will go first."

Brer Fox had just finished digging up the whole of his fine crop of potatoes. He looked up and saw a top hat and bonnet bobbing along, just showing over the top of his fence.

"I bet I could knock that top hat off," said Brer Fox. "And that bonnet too."

He picked up a large potato and aimed at the top hat. But he hit the bonnet instead and it flew up into the air. There were squeals from the other side of the fence.

Brer Fox began to giggle. "I'll get that top hat now!" he said, and aimed another large potato at it. The hat flew off, and there was a squeal of fright.

Brer Fox held his sides and laughed until he cried.

Brer Rabbit and his wife were busy picking up the two big potatoes when they saw Brer Bear coming towards them.

Quickly the rabbits hid, and watched as Brer Fox came to the gate to greet Brer Bear.

"What are you looking so pleased about, Brer Fox?" asked Brer Bear.

"Oh, Brer Bear, you should have seen me throwing my potatoes just now," laughed Brer Fox. "I saw a top hat and a bonnet bobbing along the top of the fence, and I got them both in two shots! You should have heard the squeals!"

Brer Bear picked up a potato.

"I'd like a shot too, Brer Fox. Look – there's a hat!"

One of the little rabbits was walking by the fence, his hat on a stick.

Brer Bear threw his potato but it missed.

"Bad shot!" said Brer Fox, and threw his. He knocked off the hat and roared with laughter when he heard frightened squeals from the other side of the fence.

"This is fun," said Brer Bear, and filled his pockets with potatoes. "We can pick them all up later," said Brer Fox, filling his pockets too.

Three hats bobbed along the fence, and Brer Fox and Brer Bear showered potatoes at them until all three were knocked off.

"I wish it was Brer Rabbit and his family on the other side of the fence," said Brer Fox. "It would serve him right for all the tricks he's played on me."

As Brer Rabbit strolled past the fence again, he heard Brer Fox say, "Another top hat! There must be a wedding somewhere. This is my shot!" But Brer Fox was so excited he missed altogether. Brer Bear was giggling so much that he couldn't hit it either. It took seven potatoes to knock off the top hat.

"Two more bonnets," cried Brer Fox. "Quick before they go."
Brer Fox and Brer Bear hit the bonnets with their first shots
and felt very pleased with themselves.

"Come on, top hat, I'm waiting for you!" called Brer Fox.

But no more top hats came, no more bonnets and no more caps.

Brer Rabbit and his family had filled their sacks with potatoes
and had scampered quietly home through the woods.

Brer Fox and Brer Bear waited for a while, then they took a sack and went to pick up the potatoes on the other side of the fence. But there were none to be seen.

Brer Fox was very angry indeed. "Where have all my potatoes gone?" he shouted.

"I wonder if it *was* anything to do with that rascal, Brer Rabbit?" said Brer Bear. "Let's go and pay him a visit."

A wonderful smell was coming from Brer Rabbit's house,
and Brer Fox knocked loudly at the door.

"Who's there?" cried Brer Rabbit.

"It's me," shouted Brer Fox. "Something smells good,
Brer Rabbit."

"It's soup," cried Brer Rabbit. "POTATO SOUP! But don't think you can have any!" And Brer Fox heard the noise of all the little rabbits banging their soup spoons on the table and laughing.

Brer Fox and Brer Bear walked away too angry to speak.

When they heard a tapping at the window, they turned round.
There was Brer Rabbit, wearing a top hat!

"You're a good shot, Brer Fox!" he yelled through the window, raising his top hat and grinning cheekily, before returning to enjoy his bowl of delicious potato soup.